AUDREY WOOD

SWEET DREAM PIE

WILLOBEE ST

Pictures by MARK TEAGUE

THE BLUE SKY PRESS

An Imprint of Scholastic Inc. • New York

For Pauline and William Bream — A. W.

For Laura — M. T.

THE BLUE SKY PRESS

Text copyright © 1998 by Audrey Wood
Illustrations copyright © 1998 by Mark Teague
All rights reserved.   No part of this publication may be reproduced or stored in
a retrieval system or transmitted in any form or by any means, electronic, mechanical,
photocopying, recording, or otherwise, without written permission of the publisher.
For information regarding permission, please write to: Permissions Department,
The Blue Sky Press, an imprint of Scholastic Inc.,
555 Broadway, New York, New York 10012.
The Blue Sky Press is a registered trademark of Scholastic Inc.
Library of Congress catalog number: 96-54644
10 9 8 7 6 5 4 3 2 1   8 9/9 0/0 01 02 03
ISBN: 0-590-96204-3
Printed in Singapore   46
First printing, April 1998   Designed by Kathleen Westray

It was almost dawn
on Willobee Street when Pa Brindle
lit the lantern and led Ma Brindle up to their dark attic,
to an old trunk draped in cobwebs.

"I haven't slept a wink tonight," Pa said. "I've been craving a piece of Sweet Dream Pie, just like the one you made me long ago."

"The last time I made that pie you ate too much," Ma grumbled. "And your dreams weren't sweet."

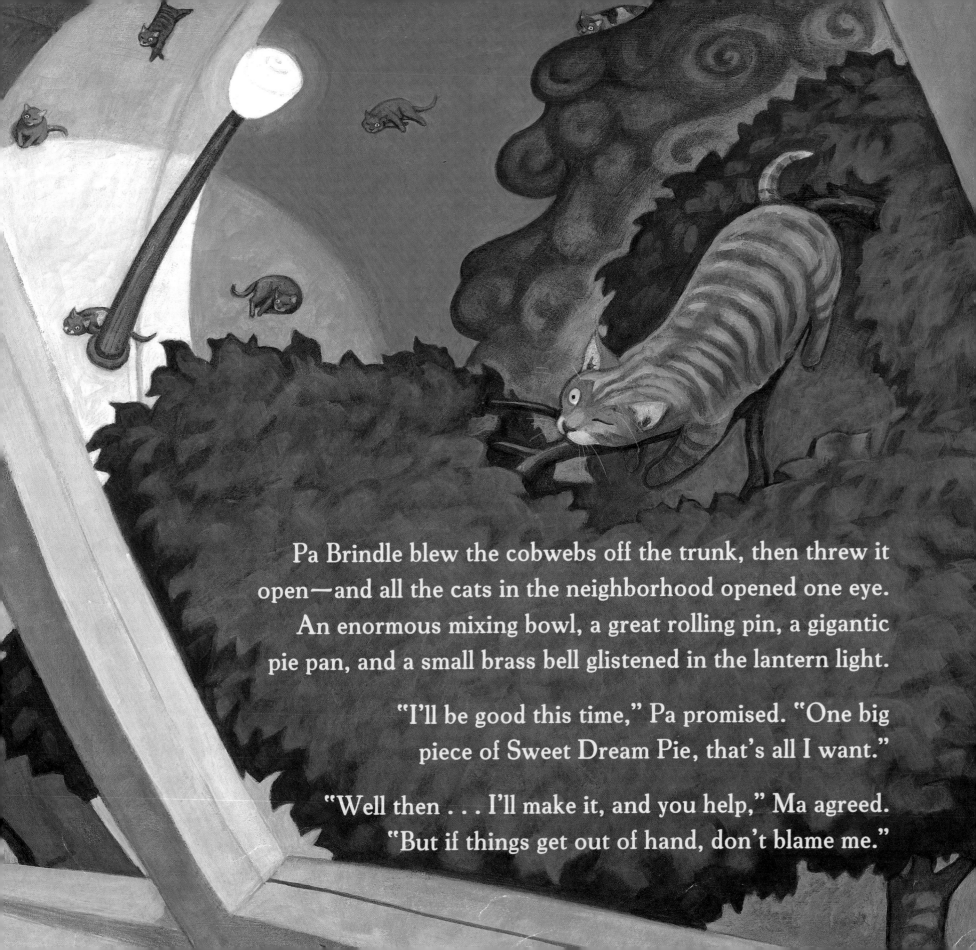

Pa Brindle blew the cobwebs off the trunk, then threw it
open—and all the cats in the neighborhood opened one eye.
An enormous mixing bowl, a great rolling pin, a gigantic
pie pan, and a small brass bell glistened in the lantern light.

"I'll be good this time," Pa promised. "One big
piece of Sweet Dream Pie, that's all I want."

"Well then . . . I'll make it, and you help," Ma agreed.
"But if things get out of hand, don't blame me."

The Brindles carried the extra-large utensils down
to the kitchen and began to make the pie. When the
dough was ready, Ma rolled it out on the table, and when
she did, all the people on Willobee Street (including little
Amy McPherson) rolled out of their beds and onto their floors.

Next, Ma fashioned two great pie crusts. Then the Brindles began to toss every sweet thing they could find into the enormous mixing bowl. Gumdrops flew through the air and rained down with marshmallows, candy corn, cinnamon hots, chewing gum, chocolate drops, butterscotch, licorice sticks, lollipops, sugar cubes, jelly beans, candy sprinkles, cookies, and more.

Clouds of powdered sugar drifted out the windows into the street.
A chocolate tornado sprang up and whirled out the door,
knocking Jonny Lunds, who was trying to deliver
newspapers, off his bicycle.

The enormous mixing bowl began to glow. A thick, sweet syrup bubbled up and oozed down the sides. The Brindles poured the filling into the giant pie pan, then wrestled the top crust into place. Ma crimped the edges, and Pa poked the steam holes. The crust began to move, as if things inside were trying to get out.

Pa shoved the pie into the oven and slammed the door.
Quickly he turned the oven dial past "bake," "broil,"
and "roast," to a setting that simply said, "special."

As the sun rose, the oven warmed, and a heat wave hit Willobee Street. It was too hot to go to work or school, so everyone stayed home, doing cool things. Even Mary Chub, who had never missed a day at the library in fifteen years, lounged beneath her sunflower.

By noon, the delicious smell of Ma Brindle's Sweet Dream Pie blanketed the neighborhood with a blissful aroma. Everyone was simply drooling to taste that pie. Even baby Robbie stuck out his tongue, thinking he could lick the sweetness from the air.

The heat wave raged on into the afternoon. It was so hot, all the air conditioners stopped working.

No one was cool except for Perry Arbuckle,
who filled the tub in his conservatory
with ice cubes and sat in it.

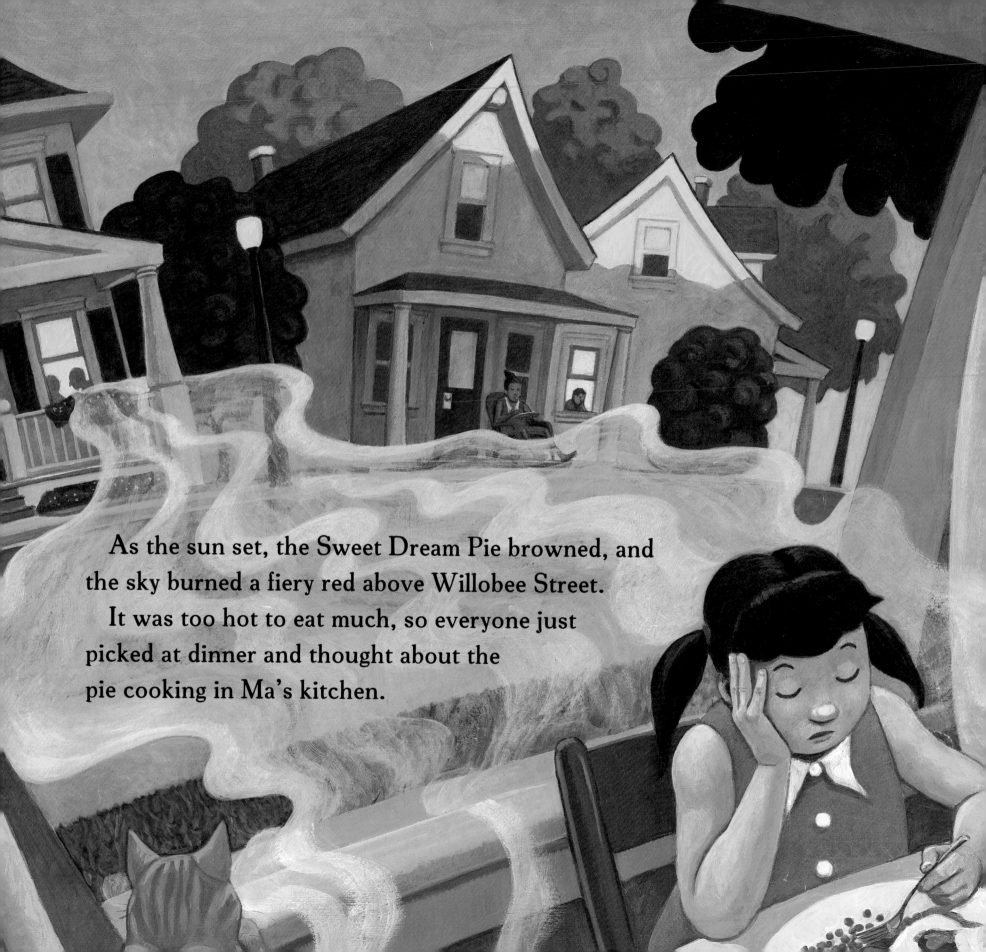

As the sun set, the Sweet Dream Pie browned, and
the sky burned a fiery red above Willobee Street.
It was too hot to eat much, so everyone just
picked at dinner and thought about the
pie cooking in Ma's kitchen.

That evening, all the neighbors found an excuse to stop by the Brindles' house. Pa set up tables and colored lights outside and invited everyone to stay and share his special dessert. They all were thrilled, except little Amy McPherson. Amy could eat no pie because it made her sneeze.

The dogs jumped up and began to chase their tails. Ma Brindle rang the small brass bell. "It's time for Sweet Dream Pie!" she called. Pa Brindle and Jonny Lunds carried the pie out and set it down.

Steam rose up from the pie, and a thick fog settled over the neighborhood. Standing side by side, the Brindles blew upon the pie to cool it. A welcome breeze sprang up, whirling napkins and party plates into the air and clearing the fog.

For the first time in thirteen hours, Willobee
Street cooled down.
Ma cut the pie as the neighbors lined up.

"Now be careful," she warned. "This pie is very rich.
One piece is all you need."

No one had ever tasted anything like Ma Brindle's
Sweet Dream Pie. It was so sweet, happy tears just rolled
down everyone's cheeks.

"Don't eat too much!" Ma kept saying. "Only one piece,
or you'll be sorry." But no one listened. They all helped
themselves to sweet thirds and fourths.

Pa Brindle broke his promise. He gobbled down sweet sixths and even sevenths. Poor Inky King ate so much he looked as if he had swallowed a bowling ball.

When Myrtle Murphy's parrot pecked up
the last crumb, a hush fell upon Willobee Street.
The neighbors thanked Ma and Pa for sharing their
wonderful pie. Suddenly all they wanted to do was go home
and snuggle in their cozy beds. Some made it, and others
dozed off along the way. Ma Brindle shook her head in dismay.

   "After all that sweetness," she said, "no one will rest well
tonight." Then she went inside to get her broom.

That's when the dreaming began. Pa Brindle's dream was the first to pop out. Bigger than a dump truck, it galloped through the neighborhood, whistling for the others to follow. Dreams of every shape, size, and color drifted up from their dreamers and began to sport and play. All of the dreamers on Willobee Street tossed and turned in their restless sleep.

Ma Brindle had never seen so many wild dreams. They were everywhere and into everything! The dreams were too happy and too excited, doing things they shouldn't do.

When enough was enough, Ma took up her broom and began to sweep, sweep, sweep, until she had swept away every last dream from Willobee Street.

All of the dreamers, including Pa Brindle, sighed with relief and finally settled in for a good night's sleep.

From her bedroom window, little Amy McPherson watched it all,
and for once in her life she was glad she could eat no pie.